Per and the Dala Horse

Rebecca Hickox
illustrated by Yvonne Gilbert

A Doubleday Book for Young Readers

A Doubleday Book for Young Readers
Published by Delacorte Press
Bantam Doubleday Dell Publishing Group, Inc.
1540 Broadway, New York, New York 10036
Doubleday and the portrayal of an anchor with a dolphin are
trademarks of Bantam Doubleday Dell Publishing Group, Inc.

Library of Congress Cataloging-in-Publication Data
Hickox, Rebecca.
Per and the Dala horse / Rebecca Hickox ; illustrated by Yvonne Gilbert.
p.   cm.
Summary: An orginal story based on Swedish folklore, in which a
young boy and his toy horse outwit the trolls after his two older
brothers have tried and failed.
ISBN 0-385-32075-2
[1. Fairy tales.   2. Trolls — Fiction.   3. Brothers — Fiction.
4. Sweden — Fiction.   5. Horses — Fiction.]   I. Gilbert, Yvonne, ill.   II. Title.
PZ8.A96Pe   1995
[E] — dc20   93–38596   CIP   AC

The text of this book is set in Cochin.
Manufactured in Italy
October 1995
10   9   8   7   6   5   4   3   2   1

Once, many years ago in the province of Dalarna, a farmer died, leaving all he owned to his three sons. To the eldest, Nils, he willed his farm, the workhorse, and the plow. To the second, Erik, he left his fine riding horse. The third son, Per, was hardly more than a boy. He received a small wooden horse, handsomely carved and painted, which some said had been given to his father by a *skogsrå*, a spirit of the forest.

Each was pleased with his portion, but Nils and Erik scoffed at Per. "What good is a little wooden horse for working a farm?" "It's enough that it's beautiful," answered Per, "and besides, it may be useful someday."

One Sunday morning when the three arrived at church, they found the congregation in an uproar and the parson wringing his hands.

"The trolls have stolen the gold communion cup from my house!" he cried. "I should never have taken it from the church for cleaning. It would have been safe here on holy ground!"

"Ten gold pieces to the one who returns it," shouted the merchant Gustav over the din.

That night Per dreamed that his wooden horse was standing on his pillow. "Take me to the trolls," it whispered in Per's ear. "I know how to get the cup back."

The next morning Per told of his dream, but Nils announced he already had a plan for retrieving the gold cup. After breakfast he hitched the workhorse to the plow and started digging long furrows from the churchyard across many fields and through the woods until he reached the foot of the trolls' mountain. After two days of plowing that way, Nils began making furrows across those he'd already dug.

At sunset on Thursday, the best night of the week to find trolls, Erik and Per walked with him to the church.

"Here," said Per, "take my little horse. Maybe he can help you."

Nils laughed. "I don't need help from a toy, for I have outwitted the trolls."

"Just remember," warned Erik, "if you drink the trolls' brew, you'll lose your memory and become their slave."

"Don't worry," said Nils, "I won't drink a drop."

He bade them farewell and strode across the fields and through the forest. He did not stop until he stood on the side of the trolls' mountain.

"Trolls!" he called. "I'm thirsty."

Now trolls are lazy creatures always hoping to capture a human to do their work, so in less than a moment the earth cracked open and a troll maiden carrying a drinking horn climbed out. "Here, sir, our special brew should quench your thirst," she said, offering him the horn.

"Ha," Nils replied, "I am a prosperous landowner. I do not drink from horns."

A second troll climbed out of the earth with a silver cup.

"You'll find our brew tastes especially good after a climb."

Nils again refused to take it. "I can drink from silver anytime. Do the trolls have nothing finer to offer a guest?"

With that a third troll emerged with the church's gold cup.

"Here is our finest," said the troll. "See how it makes the brew sparkle?"

"Ah, that's more to my liking," cried Nils. He grabbed the cup, dashed the contents at the trolls, and began running down the mountainside.

A fearsome howling rose behind him as
scores of trolls poured from the earth and gave
chase. The noise doubled when they reached
the foot of the mountain and found all the cross
furrows, for a troll cannot pass over a cross.

They can, however, run swift as a deer and never
tire. Even though the trolls had to run around every
cross, Nils was only halfway back to the church when
they caught him, gave him a terrible beating, and took
back the cup.

That night the wooden horse again appeared in Per's dream. "Troll magic can work two ways. Take me to get the cup."

The next Thursday Erik tried his luck.

"Take my wooden horse," urged Per.

"It's a real horse I'll be taking," replied Erik as he mounted his horse and started out, careful not to disturb Nils's furrows.

Erik found the same welcome and used the same trick to get the golden cup. This time, however, when he had it in his hands, he leaped astride his horse and galloped down the mountain.

The trolls again streamed after him. Though the crosses slowed them and Erik's horse was swift, two of the strongest trolls were nearly alongside as he approached the churchyard.

"The tail!" screamed the other trolls. "Grab the beast's tail!"

The closest troll did, and just outside the churchyard gate horse and rider were pulled to the ground. The angry trolls gave them a pounding, then ran back to their mountain with the cup.

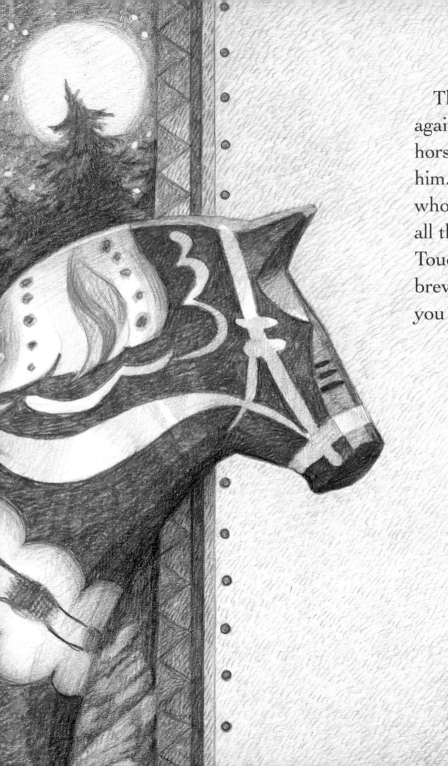

That night Per once
again dreamed that his
horse was speaking to
him. "The wood spirit
who carved me knew
all the trolls' tricks.
Touch me with their
brew, and see what
you shall see."

The next Thursday Per
announced that he was
going to rescue the cup. "My
little horse will help me," he said.
"You'll need more than a toy to
escape the trolls," warned Erik.
"They're bound to be very
angry by now."
Nils agreed. "They'll drag you
and your horse down into their
caves, and then you will need
rescuing along with the cup."

Nevertheless, that evening Per slipped his horse into his pocket and walked off across the countryside. When he was halfway up the mountain, he set his horse on the ground and called out, "Trolls! Have you anything to offer a thirsty traveler?"

A suspicious troll appeared through a crack in the earth and held out a drinking horn.

"No, thank you," said Per. "Horns are too common."

When a second troll offered him a silver cup, he waved it away.

"Silver is not to my liking."

The trolls did not want to chase the communion cup again. They formed a ring around Per before a troll maiden finally came forward holding the precious gold cup. As soon as it was in his hands, Per poured a few drops of the enchanted brew on the little horse. In an instant it stood as tall as a stallion. Clutching the cup, Per leaped to its back. The horse bounded over the circle of trolls and galloped down the mountain. With a roar of rage the trolls raced after them.

As Per and his horse approached the churchyard, the two strongest trolls caught up. They reached out to seize the horse's tail but found only smooth wood and shiny paint. Though they scratched and clawed, there was no tail to grab. Per clutched the cup with one arm and the horse's neck with the other as they flew over the wall and landed in a leap on holy ground. Underworld magic had no power there. The little horse lay on its side, a toy as before except for several deep scratches along its flanks.

With his ten gold pieces Per bought a small farm
and soon added to it. In the years that followed he
became one of the wealthiest farmers in the province,
but his most cherished possession remained a
scratched wooden horse, which he proudly left to
his youngest son.

Dala horses, *dalahästen*, are hand-carved, brightly painted toys that have been made in the Dalarna province of Sweden for over 150 years. I purchased one in the Swedish-American town of Lindsborg, Kansas, several years ago, and right away that little horse begged to be in a story. In search of the right one, I read hundreds of traditional Swedish tales, but none had a Dala horse. I did, however, find a story called "Retrieving the Cup" in John Lindow's *Swedish Legends and Folktales*. In this story an enterprising young man rescues a communion cup by plowing crosses and cutting his horse's mane and tail so that the trolls won't have anything to grab. This seemed to me to be the perfect situation for a Dala horse with its painted mane and tail. The story as recorded is quite short, so in addition to adding my little horse, I also changed it to a traditional "three brothers" tale. Although this is now more an original story than the true retelling of a folktale, I have included several themes that appear frequently in Swedish tales, such as the power of the church against otherworldly creatures, Thursday being the best night to find trolls, and the trolls' constant attempts to enslave humans.